Into The Mountains Mountains I Look

D1516237

By: Madisen M. Bourman

Printed in the United States of America

First Printing, 2018

10 9 8 7 6 5 4 3 2

ISBN: 978-1983579950

Dedicated to:

My heavenly Father

and

My Aunt Carolyn,

"May there be pain in the night, but joy comes in the morning."

Psalms 30:5

In Memory of:

Charles Melford Brenden

'Papa Chuck'

&

Alice Ann Brenden

Acknowledgments:

Writing this book was no walk in the park. I could have not done it without my Father's guidance. God has taught me much as I've worked on this book, He is the reason I write.

I would like to thank my Dad and Mom for all of the time and effort they have put into my life and raising me to be who I am. My parents have encouraged me to do what I love and try hard. They are my biggest encouragement and they are always there to look at what I am writing. I would also like to thank my two brothers, Randy and Chas, and my sister, Miranda. They have given me ideas and listened to me talk on and on about my book and helped with editing and feedback. I love them all so dearly.

A huge THANK YOU to my beta readers! My book would not be where it is without each of you. All seven of you have helped so very much. So, thank you, Amalia Kastner, Amanda Hage, Havala Schoenfelder, Kate Muntean, Carleigh Trout, Tami Bourman, and Robert Bourman.

Sincerely,

-Madisen M. Bourman

Introduction:

Hello there!

My name is Zipporah Ann Foxton. I live with my Pa, Ma, and seven siblings. I heard you were wondering what my life is like? Well, I am about to tell you all about it and what happens in my day to day life in the early 1900s. Oh, you are wondering where I live? I live in Townsend, Tennessee, it is pretty small. But I really love it! Come on! Let's go for an adventure!

-Let The-

Adventure

-Begin-

Chapter One

Footsteps approached the bed, I opened my eyes to see my sister, Eliza, staring at me.

"Wake uh-p, Zippy!"

"It's not morning yet, is it?" I replied as I turned over and pulled the thick blankets back over my head.

"It sure is! And it's Saturday, you know what that means— pancakes for breakfast!" Eliza ran out of our room.

I sat up and looked around our small, but cozy bedroom. I share a room with my four other sisters. Amelia, who we call Mel, is the oldest girl, Esther, Zipporah (that's me!), Lynn, and Eliza. We all have very different personalities. For instance, like me, I am more laid back then Mel, Esther, Lynn, and Eliza. On the other hand, Eliza is the one to have her own opinion and stick with it, she won't change her mind. Lynn is more of a listener than the rest of us talkers, she and Eliza clash heads with ideas, mainly because Eliza won't see other's ideas. Esther is very quiet, she is more of a follower. Mel tells it like it is. She also listens to everyone's ideas, hopes, and dreams. Mel and I have always been so close growing up, that has changed a bit in the past few months now that she has her "special" friend, Paul Westly around.

With another shout from downstairs, I slipped out of our double bed, made my side and got ready for breakfast.

My little brothers, Leigh and Thomas were already sitting at the table with their forks in hand. Leigh and Thomas have always been the closest of anyone in our family. Being close in age, they are almost like twins. They look alike, act alike, talk alike, and even dress alike. My brothers have wild imaginations and they love adding Eliza into their adventures, I think mainly because they need a damsel in distress.

The noise of my family chatting filled the air as the sweet smell of pancakes fumed around.

Sitting down at the table my family bowed their heads as Pa, who was sitting at the head of the table, said the blessing for the meal.

"Lord, thank you for this meal and for the hands that prepared it. Bless our family and bless our son Liam and his new wife, Emily, as they are newlyweds and come back from their honeymoon.

In Jesus' name, Amen."

My brother, Liam, just got married in February to Emily Nicole Westly. They had not gone on their honeymoon yet because they wanted to have better weather. They went camping in the mountains. I am sure it was beautiful! I wish I could have gone with...

As I started to eat my breakfast, I looked at my Pa, his reddish-brown hair was in a slick fashion. All of my brothers look just like him. Ma always had cut all the boys' hair, but now I have taken over that responsibility. I have enjoyed taking on this new learning experience. Ever since I was a little girl, I have always dreamed of running my own household and having my own children's hair to cut. Seeing Mel getting close with Paul makes me want to get married soon. I often have to remind myself that I need to trust in God and His timing. All I want is to meet a God-honoring man who is firm but gentle, loves children as much as I do, handsome and on the taller side, and who will love me no matter the problem and bring me closer to Jesus.

We finished breakfast and went onto cleaning. Saturday is family chore day, the most dreaded day of the week for all of us.

Straightening my back from scrubbing the floor, I saw Leigh and Thomas covered head to toe in mud.

"Heh-hey Zippy." Thomas whispered with a slight grin.

"Don't you dare step off that rug. Maybe Esther can help you..." my voice trailed off in a huff. Swallowing hard Leigh gave out a yell for

Esther, fearing that he was going to get a scolding for playing in the mud.

"Esther, can you please come here?"

Eliza was the first in the room, even though she was not called. Her personality was, hmm, motherly? Yes, we will call it that.

"Mother is going to be so upset with you," Eliza smirked. Being only twelve, she always has too much to say.

"My, my..." Esther walked in and shook her head. I quickly slipped out of the room for a little bit of quiet. Most of the time Liam, Mel, and Esther were in charge of the younger kids when Ma and Pa were gone out working or helping a neighbor, but now that Liam got married, it's up to Mel, Me, and Esther—and it is not always easy.

When I was young, we would stay home with Liam and he would teach us about bears and deer—his two favorite animals. Ma was gone about two days a week helping our neighbors with baking or taking care of little children whose mothers needed help.

~~~

I walked out the back door to the garden to grab a couple tomatoes for supper as a horse approached me. The man I saw was scruffy and had a slim frame. Not recognizing my own brother was not something to be proud of. They had been gone for two and a half weeks.

"Liam? You're back!"

"Course I am! Didn't you think I would be?" He jumped off his horse and gave me a gentle hug as we walked back to the house. Liam has a strong upper body build. He gives the most wonderful hugs, I had forgotten about how I missed his hugs. Liam is a very affectionate person, especially to us girls. While he was still at home, he would hug us all before going off to work. I knew he would always make a great husband for some lucky lady.

After the great reunion, I headed back outside to finish the job I started out to do in the first place. I thought about how strange it will be not to have Liam here anymore. His new wife, Emily Nicole was compassionate and kind. Our families were always very close, I don't know how I never saw this relationship blossom... my thoughts jumped as I searched for the perfect bright red tomatoes.

Feeling satisfied with my selection, I set down my basket and sat in the heat as sweat started rolling down my face. *Oh, what a joy to have such a big garden...* my thoughts were cut off by Mel yelling for me,

"Zipporah! Hurry! We need the tomatoes for supper." Mel is gentle and always honest, but also will tell you like it is—and I like that. I quickly jumped up from the large stump I was sitting on and walked to the house.

The stump in the garden had been there for as long as I could remember. The stump holds so many memories of when I was little and it was a tree, I would wrap my little fingers around the ropes on the swing as Liam would stand behind me and push me. I would yell in delight and encourage him to push me higher and higher. I thought I'd maybe make it to the moon if I went high enough. Sadly, the tree was taken out by a big storm when I was twelve. I'm glad I can still enjoy a part of the tree.

I continued on to the house. We live on the outskirts of Townsend, Tennessee. There are not many people who live here. Most of the houses look like ours. My family's home is a small light wooden house, the logs are very weathered from years of sun and storms, but it is very beautiful to me. It may not be beautiful to others, but for my family, it has so many memories and stories in the walls of our home. It is the house I've grown up in. I came through the door to see my mother, Mel, Esther, Lynn, and Eliza hustling around the kitchen.

"Sorry, I got distracted" I explained.

"It's all right. Here, get busy." My mother had just gotten back from helping our elderly neighbor make jam. She handed me a knife to cut up the tomatoes I had been sent to get. I looked at her with confusion.

"What's this for?"

"The tomatoes..." she had a puzzled look, as did I.

"Oh no! I left them outside in the garden, I'll go get them!" Embarrassed from already taking too much time I had forgot my assignment! *I can't get anything right lately—I keep forgetting everything!* Most people think I am childlike and immature, I've even been told that! I do forget things often and mess up. I guess maybe one day I'll grow up.

Chapter Two

Holding out his hand, my ten-year-old brother Thomas helped us ladies into the carriage.

"Don't you just love Sundays?" Lynn looked at me with a sigh of relief.

"They're very nice," I took a deep breath as I tried to get used to Mel's church dress she "let" me have. It was rather tight and flattering, but I can hardly breathe in it. I was just told to wear it so I am. The rest of the ride was somewhat quiet. I think everyone was just enjoying the crisp morning air and the birds chirping. Tennessee is known for the rolling hills and beautiful landscape. I watched as we passed Little River. I saw a little boy in his Sunday clothes watching the fish. I could see him unstrap his shoes, slip off his socks, and stand at the edge of the river to get his toes wet. A mischievous look spread across his face. I laughed to myself as his young mother came and pulled him away, collecting his shoes and socks, they headed to their wooden house beside the river.

The bell rang as we approached the church. Every Sunday the ladies get out of the carriage and the men go to tie up the horses and unhitch the carriage, then, we meet back inside the church.

Pastor Cecil opened his bible to Joshua 1:9 and talked about being strong and courageous. Pastor Cecil continued throughout his message walking back and forth across the front of the sanctuary in a relaxed way.

Once church was over, I slipped over to where the Westly family was standing. Eva Westly stood by her brother Paul, who was talking to my sister, Mel.

"Thought you'd be over here!"

"Oh! Of course, I was just about to come find you!" Eva smiled.

"Are we still on for the horse ride later?" I questioned our previously made plans.

"Oh, I hope so!" Eva smiled.

"Zipporah! Time to go!" Hearing Thomas' voice I said goodbye and walked to the carriage.

"Lynn, you're wrong, dandelions are white and then yellow," Eliza stated being as stubborn as always.

"It's yellow first, ask Zippy!" Lynn looked at me with her eyebrows raised.

"Mm, Lynn's right." I didn't really want to be in this discussion so I diluted it quickly. I mean, who fights about the color of flowers?

After lunch I helped clean up and went to the barn. Jumping on my horse, I headed north to the Westly's house. I approached their barn just when Eva came out on her cream Boulonnais horse, Harry.

"Ready?" I clicked my tongue and off we went through the woods.

"It sure is beautiful this time of year!" Eva whispered in amazement, the dead leaves from last winter were blowing around in the wind. Their colors were faded and they were hard and dry. I wished they were colorful and awaiting some young children to come and play with them. Eva likes how it looks now, but I don't think so.

We were simply riding along, enjoying our ride and, out of nowhere, two people passed us on horses creating a cloud of dust for us to choke on.

"Who was that? That was so rude!" I asked as I watched them. *I'm going to find out...* I started galloping toward them. They were slowing down and I glanced back to see Eva hot on my heels.

"Excuse me, that's not the way you should ride around people." I shook my head. The people's heads bobbed up and down with laughter, but due to all the dust, their faces remained a mystery.

"Who are you?" Curiosity got the best of Eva. All the sudden, it hit me like a door. I knew that laugh!

"Liam… Emily..." I rolled my eyes.

"Thought we would play a little game." Liam laughed at us.

"Not funny!" I said lightly. We all enjoyed the rest of the ride home together.

Once we arrived home, I got busy with doing my chores. Since Pa started working at the sawmill for a higher income, he doesn't have much time for the animals. I first had to go to the root cellar and get the leftover milk from this morning to bring in the house when I was done with tonight's milking. I opened the door, grabbed the pail, and turned to go back out. I forgot that there were new potato bins by the door and tripped over one. *NO! Not the milk!* I quickly jumped back to my feet after my body hit the ground. I had spilt the milk. I collected my thoughts and went to the barn. I walked over to pet our cow, Maple, she turned her head to see me, a small framed lady, with two loose braids. Maple is very particular about who milks her, and she doesn't like when I do it. I sat down just as Leigh came out to the barn.

"What are you doing, Zip?" Leigh questioned with a puzzled face.

"I'm trying to milk Maple." I said with a puff still looking for the Udder.

"Huh... that's a bull calf." Leigh laughed at my stupidity.

"I knew that." I didn't really. "Then where is Maple?"

"Over there." He pointed across the barn.

"Got it!" I stood up and started for 'over there' and not watching where I was going, I hit the empty milk pail and, once again, fell to the ground. *I've had enough!* At that moment, Pa walked in. I kept on across the barn, not ready to face him yet and not ready to give up, I sat down to milk Maple. And of course, she was not cooperating with me, she kept hitting me with her tail and lifting her foot.

"Pa, do you have a second?" I approached him.

"Sure, sweetie, what do you need?" Pa's tired, blue eyes looked at me.

"I was going to milk Maple and I accidentally tripped in the root cellar and spilled all of the milk, I'm sorry" I looked at pa.

"It's okay, at least we have milk from this morning,"

"I spilt this morning's milk," I admitted "I fell twice, once in the root cellar, and once in the barn, I tried milking Maple after that and she wouldn't let me touch her." Pa was silent for a minute.

"I'll come help you." He stopped what he was doing and showed me. Finally, after a few weeks I can milk her all alone.

One day when I was milking Maple, Mel came out and sat next to me.

"Can we talk for a second?" She smiled at me.

"Yeah, what is it?" I continued milking Maple.

"Paul Westly asked Pa for his blessing to marry me!" I stopped and looked at her with a pleased face.

"What?" I jumped up, "I'm so excited for you! I can't believe it!" We sat and talked for quite a while about Paul and Mel's wedding and what life was going to be like without her around.

Chapter Three

I peeked out my window and saw the sun shining over the field. I decided on a deep blue skirt and white shirt to wear for today. I just finished making it and washed it a few days ago, I've been waiting to finally wear my new outfit.

"Morning!" I yelled as I came down the stairs to see my parents and another couple turn their heads to look at who was coming down the stairs.

"Morning sweetheart," Pa said, "this is Mr. and Mrs. Taylor, they just moved in about a mile down the road," He turned to the Taylors "This is my daughter, Zipporah." He motioned for me to come sit down.

"Nice to meet you, Miss Zipporah, I'm Tucker Taylor and this is my wife Mollie." Mr. Taylor's scruffy face was slim and his beard was chestnut brown, he had a look to him that was slightly scary, he looked me up and down with a sweeping glance. It was not the most flattering look to give someone!

"Nice to meet you too." I smiled at our new neighbors.

"We might just have a daughter your age, I'm sure she would love if you went over there and introduced yourself." Mrs. Taylor commented with a smile.

"I'll eat and head to your house." I said as I excused myself from our company.

Why did I agree to this? I don't even know these people. I thought as I walked to the Taylor's house, *Lord, please help me to be kind and help me to be a friend.*

I lifted my hand to the wooden door to knock as it just flew open. Before I knew what was happening, I was splashed with dirty sink water. I stood there and wiped my eyes away to see who very carelessly splashed me, he was a tall man with cloudy blue eyes, dark brown hair, and wide shoulders.

"I'm so sorry." He was as shocked as I was.

"It's all right," I swallowed hard. "I'll just go home now," I turned and hurried away before he could say anything else. *What was I thinking? Ah! And on my new, beautiful, clean outfit!* I walked into the house and Thomas and Eliza looked at me.

"What happened to you?" Eliza and Thomas started laughing. At the noise of their laughter, Mel came in.

"I know, I know. I'm dripping wet." I stated as I trudged up the stairs. Quickly changing out of my sopping wet, beautiful shirt and skirt, I changed into an old, clean, dry dress.

"So what happened?" Mel came in and sat on the side of the bed.

"I went to our new neighbor's house and as soon as I went to knock, a childish man threw a large bucket of dirty, soapy water at me. Ugh!" I lifted my fists to my hips.

"Calm down, Zipporah. I'm sure it was just an accident!" Mel always seemed to calm me down.

"I'm sure it was," I flopped down on the bed. "I'm so embarrassed!" Mel looked at my pitiful frown.

"Come on, let's take your mind off the water accident and go for a walk, maybe to Liam and Emily's house!"

The walk was wonderful, until we entered Liam's barn. There stood the man who splashed me with the dirty dish water. I looked at him, he looked at me.

"Ah, Matthias, these are my sisters, Amelia and Zipporah." Liam said as he saddled his horse.

"Nice to meet you," Matthias paused, "again. Sorry 'bout that, didn't see ya standing there before, you know, when I drenched you."

"You did what?" Liam broke out in laughter and Mel joined him. I glanced at

Matthias to see if he was laughing, he blushed and turned to Liam who had finally stopped laughing. *Could this get any more awkward?* I asked myself.

"Well, we are going to see Emily…" Mel and I quickly left the barn.

"Emily! Are you home?" I said as I walked in to their house.

"Yeah, just hold on!" She came out, as pale as ever and looked exhausted.

"Are you okay?" I asked.

"I've been sick lately…" Her voice trailed off.

"With?" The word slipped out of my mouth as Mel elbowed into my side. I was being rather too nosy.

"Well, we wanted to tell everyone together, but I don't think that is going to work now. It is just morning sickness." She smiled at us.

"Seriously?!?!" I screamed as Mel and I ran towards her! The room was filled with excitement and laughter.

"When are you due?" Mel questioned the soon to be mommy.

"Sometime in December. Now don't tell anyone, it's still a secret!" Liam and Matthias walked in and made it slightly awkward, again.

"Well, we better go. Bye!" I quickly got out of their house and back onto the dirt road with Mel.

~~~

"Zipporah, your father and I are going into town for some supplies for the mill. Esther and Mel are coming along to help us, so that means you and Lynn will hold down the fort. I'll leave a list for you, we will only be gone for two or three days." Mother sat down at the table and started writing a list.

"Okay. Lynn and I can handle it." I nodded my head.

"We will leave in the morning, so I need you to be awake when we leave." *ugh...getting up early? One of my most hated things...*

Morning came too quickly and I had to get up.

"Here is the list; take care of your siblings and don't burn the house down." Ma smiled at me and went out the door. *What a list! It's huge!*

To do list:

1. Make the meals
2. Clean up after meals and wash dishes
3. Keep your siblings clean
4. Have your siblings bathed Saturday night
5. Milk the cows, collect the eggs, feed the pigs, clean the horse pen, and feed the goats
6. Saturday is cleaning day!
   -wash the floors
   -do the laundry
   -wash the windows
   -sweep around the fireplace
   -dust the furniture
   -pick up bedrooms

Liam and Emily will pick you up for church, make sure you have everyone ready.

This is going to be a couple "easy days..." I thought as I made oatmeal for the rest of the family that was home. I looked out the window and thought, *I love the mountains...with the sunshine...over the barn...God is so good. What better time than now to go and read the bible?* I finished the oatmeal and left a note by it:

Lynn and Eliza,

I made breakfast and I'm going out to read for a bit, I'll be back soon. Make sure the boys eat all of their oatmeal, I know they don't like it very much.

-Zipporah

I grabbed my Bible and slipped out the back door. *The morning air is so refreshing...* I walked a ways and found a large rock to sit on, I opened up to my favorite verse. Psalms 121: 1-2. **I lift up my eyes to the mountains—where does my help come from? My help comes from the Lord, the Maker of heaven and earth.**

Chapter Four

I walked into the house. It was spotless and breakfast was cleaned up. *Well, this is not what I expected...* I thought as I turned the corner to see Lynn reading to the rest of the siblings.

"Good job on cleaning up." I sat next to Leigh on the couch,

"The kids really helped." Lynn smiled at me. *Huh, she really is growing up.*

"What chores need to be done now?" I stood up and started toward the kitchen.

"We did them all," Thomas said proudly. "Can we go to the creek?"

"Oh... this is what you wanted, I suppose we can go down there for a while." Shouts of joy filled the house. I packed lunch and off we went to the creek for a refreshing swim. My siblings splashed in the water and I decided to join them,

"It is so refreshing on a hot day like this!" I laughed.

"Sure is!" Eliza splashed me. We swam for a while and then went to eat our picnic.

"Mm—peanut butter and grape jelly sandwiches always taste so good, especially on hot summer days." Eliza stated as she stuffed the last bite in her mouth. Leigh and Thomas were over in the bushes and they started yelling,

"ZIPPORRRRRRAH!!!!!! We found something you might like!" I jumped up and quickly went to the bushes.

"Blueberries?!?!" I was simply delighted! "Let's go get the picnic basket and start picking them so we can make a pie!"

The sun was hot on my shoulders and I could feel my face burning.

"It's so hot out, Zip, can we be done?" Leigh's hazel eyes looked up at me. "I think we have enough, come on!"

"Woo hoo…" His cheers were quickly cut off by someone else picking blueberries.

"A b-b-bear!" Leigh stood still, as did I. *Oh no! The rest of the children are behind me a ways… but we are right in harm's way!*

"Stay still, Leigh, don't make any sudden movements." I warned him. All of the sudden, little Leigh started talking.

"God wouldn't want you to hurt my sister, don't tell anyone but she is my favorite so leave her alone!"

Warmed and frightened by what my brother said, I just stood there. The bear apparently understood and walked into the woods.

"Well, he is gone." Leigh went on with walking out of the bushes. I stood there and shook my head, *what just happened?* I could not believe it. "Are you coming?" Leigh asked me as he took my hand. "Don't worry, I'll keep you safe." I held onto his hand and we walked home with the rest of the bunch.

~~~

"Mm—it smells like blueberry pie!" My little brother Thomas hollered from the kitchen table. "Do we get to sample any?"

"Not right now, Thomas, but soon. You don't want to spoil your supper, do you?" I looked at him with a smile.

"I don't get that, how would I spoil my supper with pie?" Thomas questioned.

"If you eat pie, you won't be hungry, now will you?" He sat quietly, showing that I proved my point.

"Yee-Haw! I'm a cowboy and I fight outlaws!" Leigh chased screaming Eliza.

"Whoa!" I stepped in front of them. "Are the outlaw and cowboy hungry for supper?" Whoops and hollers filled the kitchen. We sat around the table and Leigh volunteered to pray.

"Lord, I thank you for this meal and bless the hands that prepared it. Thank you for keeping us safe from the bear. And keep Pa, Ma, Mel, and Esther safe. Amen." Leigh smiled as everyone stared at him.

"A bear?" Eliza questioned.

"Yeah, I'll tell you the story when we eat pie." We finished supper and the kids were impatiently waiting to hear about Leigh's bear story.

"So, Zip and I were walking around in the bushes picking berries, and out of nowhere, a bear jumped out at us! I scared the bear away and he ran, frightened." My sibling's eyes were large. Leigh had completed his mission, to scare my siblings.

"Is that true, Zipporah?" Lynn questioned.

"Yes, it is." Everyone was silent, so I went and started washing the dishes.

"Can we go out and play?" Eliza asked.

"Um—yes, take your siblings and I'll finish up the dishes. I smiled at the foursome, as hand-in-hand they skipped together.

A knock came to the back door, *I wonder who that is…* I opened the door to see. *Ugh! Why is he here?* "Hello Matthias, what can I do for you?" I faked a smile.

"Hi Zipporah, is your pa home?"

"No, he had to go into town for a couple days. He will be back sometime tomorrow. Is there something I can do to help?" I tried to be kind.

"No, it was just some business we have to discuss. Thanks for the offer anyways. And Zipporah, I'm sorry for the first time we met, it was an accident. Will you forgive me?" He asked with his straw hat in his hands. *Ah? Why can't I be nice to him? He is a nice guy!*

"Yes, I accept your apology. Thank you." I actually gave him a real smile this time.

"I better get going, see you tomorrow at church." He put his hat on and went out the back door.

"Who was that?" Lynn disturbed my thoughts. *Pull yourself together!*

"Um—that was Matthias Taylor, they moved in about a mile from us. Why?" An awkward silence filled the room.

"No, reason." Lynn turned and ran up the stairs. *Humph…*

Chapter Five

"Hurry up! Liam and Emily will be here shortly!" I yelled up the stairs to my four younger siblings. Eliza ran down the stairs; she held up two dresses, one light green with white little flowers and lace, and the other a purple silk dress.

"Which one?" she questioned.

"The purple one. It will match your light blonde hair and blue eyes."

"Thanks!" She turned and ran up the stairs. We waited and waited for Liam and Emily. The time grew longer and longer. We sat and waited. We heard a buggy pull up. I jumped up, but it was not Liam. It was Mr. and Mrs. Taylor and their family.

"Liam sent us to get you. Emily was feeling under the weather and he could not leave her. Hopefully she is not getting sick." Mr. Taylor stated. *I know why she sick…* I thought.

"Okay, come on, children." Their buggy was large, but they have eight kids, so it was pretty tight.

"I don't think you have met yet." Mrs. Taylor added with," This is, Peter, Matthias, Ella, Daisy, Nicole, Noah, Walter, and Lucille. And this is Zipporah, Lynn, Eliza, Thomas, and Leigh." Us children got along right away. It felt like we had been friends forever. I was sitting next to Ella, she had long, thick brown hair and had a great personality. We talked and talked, she was the same age as I.

"What's your favorite thing to do?" She asked me.

"I love walks, especially in the winter. What about you?"

"I love baking and sewing." Our conversation was filled with laughter.

Pa, Ma, Esther, and Mel got home late Sunday night.

"You did a great job on keeping the house in good shape. I'm proud of you kids!"

"They did most of the chores Saturday morning. I was surprised, but they wanted to go swimming, so that's what we did. You'll have to ask Leigh to tell you a scary story about this weekend, it's very interesting!" I laughed.

"I will when I go to say goodnight to the boys." Ma kissed my forehead and I went up to the girl's room. It was so good to have Mel and Esther back. They told us about their trip and we told them what happened at home while they were gone.

"And the bear just ran?" Mel asked.

"Yes, I was so surprised. It was cute of Leigh, but if the bear didn't get scared and run, he could have done something bad." I crawled into bed next to Eliza.

"I had a really fun few days with you in charge. It was really fun!" Eliza blinked her blue eyes.

"I had fun too, I'm very grateful for all the work you guys did." I smiled and turned over.

Morning broke and I could hear Liam and Pa talking downstairs.

"Morning!" I walked down the stairs.

"Morning, Zip!" Liam cheerfully said.

"What are you doing?" I looked at the building plans on the table.

"We are building a barn at Liam's house maybe next weekend." Pa told me.

"Huh, that will be fun!" I sat down at the table to watch them. *I like watching them, it's entertaining…*

"Pa, could you help me build something. But you can't say anything to Ma." Liam got a big grin on his face.

"Yeah, what is it?" Pa asked. Liam looked at me as he pulled a piece of paper out of his pocket.

"A crib? For what?" Pa looked confused.

"Your grandbaby." Liam's eyes were sparkling. Pa broke out in laughter! Liam gave out a loud laugh and hugged Pa.

"Emily told Zippy and Mel the other day. We are gonna tell the rest of the family soon."

"Ah! I'm so happy!" Pa gleamed. "When is she due?"

"Around the beginning of December."

"You just made my day…"

Chapter Six

The hot summer sun beat down on me and the men working on the barn. Liam had Pa, Matthias, Peter, Paul, and Mr. Taylor working on the barn. I stood watching them as they put up the large beams and started on the roof.

"Enjoying yourself?" Matthias asked me, pulling me out of the daze I was in.

"Uh—yeah. Are you having a good time, Matthias?" I asked.

"Yes, I enjoy working on these kinds of things, and I also enjoy working with your family." Matthias replied. The way he looked at people, so intently, so deep, he just felt like an honest, good man.

I walked up to Liam and Emily's house after Matthias was needed again. Mel and Lynn came over to help prepare food for the hard-working men.

"Are you just watching them?" Lynn teased.

"Yes, it's so hot out there. I better bring them some water." I started walking to the well.

"For Matthias?" Lynn teased me.

"That's inappropriate and unrealistic. Don't talk that way." I snapped at her. I got the water and walked down to the barn.

"Just what we wanted. Thanks, Zip." Pa wiped the sweat from his face.

They worked until sundown and then we had supper. The men praised the food that was prepared. A good hearty meal was in order after all of their work. It tasted so delicious. I had my plate full with steak, potatoes and gravy, fresh green beans, and a biscuit. I had kept my eye on Matthias, watching him take a plate full and sit town by Liam and start talking about who knows what! They had become very good friends and Matthias had taught my brother many things about working on the railroad and had told him many stories about the states he had visited before coming here. Later on, a large fire was built and we sat laughing and talking into the night.

"Well, girls, we better get going home. See you tomorrow at church." Pa stood up from the bench he and Liam were sitting on.

"Thanks for all the help!" Liam shook Pa's hand.

Morning came and off we went for church. Mel's wedding was six days away. The wedding was going to be in the church so that was the last Sunday to get the church ready. After church our two families talked with the pastor about what the couple wanted. *Mel is happy with Paul, that means I have to be happy for her.* I thought about her moving out of the house and how it is sad for me, we are extremely close. I watched Mel slip her hand into Paul's hand. All she talked about was Paul. She loved him and he loved her.

After leaving church, Pa and Ma dropped us off at Paul and Mel's new house to organize her stuff.

"Paul will be here very soon." Mel started pulling things out of boxes.

"Okay." I walked up the stairs, I had only been in the house once, so I wanted to explore, I turned the corner to what would be Paul and Mel's bedroom. It had a mattress up against the wall under the window and a large oak dresser on the other wall. It was very simple, but Paul and Mel are very simple people. They are both quiet around others but can have a lot of fun just one on one.

"Mel! You here?" Paul walked in and slipped out of his shoes. *I better go down and chaperone.* I thought.

"Hello, Paul." I smiled at my soon-to-be brother-in-law. I helped Mel put things away. She happily hummed the hymn, *Amazing Grace,* her voice was soft and she dreamed of the days to come.

44

"Mel, do you want a rocking chair in the living room?" Paul asked his soon to be bride.

"Oh, I have not thought about that. That would be very nice, thank you!" Mel's eyes smiled. Watching my sister be so happy made me want to get married, *In God's time.* I had to remind myself.

"It's sad you are leaving, but I'm happy for you." I confessed to my closest sister.

"I will miss being at home, it will be extremely different not having as many people around. And don't hesitate on coming and talking to me, I'll always be here for you." Mel hugged me.

"Thanks Mel!"

~~~

The day was here, Paul and Mel's wedding; September thirteenth. I walked into our room to see my beautiful sister in her pure white wedding dress with lace at the cuffs and bottom. She had two bridesmaids, Esther and I. Our lavender purple dresses were laid out on my bed.

"Wow, you look beautiful." My eyes watered up. Mel walked over and hugged me. I slipped my dress on and gave a spin for Mel.

"Beautiful, you'll have a husband before you know it." She joyfully laughed at me as I blushed.

The rest of the morning went by in a swoosh. Tears were shed by most of my family members. I remember it just like yesterday that we were all little kids and how Mel and I used Leigh and Thomas as our live baby dolls. Our favorite game was house. Liam and Esther were always the parents and the rest of us were the children, except for Eliza. We made her be the dog. Not only had Liam moved out, but now Mel too, it was just so different. I missed the days when we were kids and would all be together. Now, I am a bridesmaid at Paul and Mel's wedding.

This is happening, I am walking down the aisle, I am so nervous. Liam and Stephen (Paul's brother) were the groomsmen. I tightly gripped Liam's arm. I was frightened, *I don't like when people watch me.* Everyone in the crowd stood for Mel and Pa coming down the aisle. She looked so happy, so in love, and so full of joy. They made it to the end of the aisle and Pa gave one of his daughters away to another man. Mel's hands slid into Paul's and they smiled the biggest smiles I think I have ever seen. The Pastor started with;

"Family and Friends, we gather here today in honor of Paul John Westly and Amelia Joy Foxton's marriage.

I listened as our Pastor continued with his encouragement to the bride and groom and watched with excitement as they exchanged vows and rings.

With a smile, Pastor finished the ceremony with, "You may kiss your bride, Paul." It was slightly strange to see Mel kiss Paul for the first time...

"I now pronounce Mr. and Mrs. Paul John Westly!" The crowd cheered and the new couple ran down the aisle. The wedding party quickly followed the Groom and Bride.

"Praise God, what a wonderful wedding! Plus, that was so fun!" Esther declared. Paul and Mel were behind the church getting ready to go. Everyone came out from the church to bid the new couple away farewell for their honeymoon.

"That dress is beautiful on you, Zip!" Emily said to me.

"Thanks Em, how are you feeling?"

"Alright," she laughed and rubbed her belly.

"That's good." I smiled at my sister-in-law.

"Liam and I were wondering if you would come and stay with us for a couple days before I have our baby, to help keep up on chores and help the house get ready." Emily asked.

"Yes! Of course!" I love spending time with my siblings, one on one. I finished talking to Emily and turned to walk away,

"Hello, Zipporah!" Matthias ran up to me.

"Hi." I cheerfully greeted at the sight of Matthias.

"My parents were wondering if your family wanted to come over for supper?" He questioned.

"I'm sure they will say yes, why don't you go ask my Ma? I believe she is still in the church." I smiled and with a tilt of his hat, he was off.

~~~

"Thank you for supper, it was delicious!" Ma told Mollie Taylor as they did the dishes. Ella turned to me,

"Want to go on a walk?"

"You know me too well, that's what I wanted to do!" I laughed at her. We were just about to go out the door and when Esther requested to come along, and Matthias, and Peter. We walked a ways into the woods and Ella suggested we play hide and seek. We all agreed and Ella was it. So, we all hid, I found a couple large rocks to hide behind. All of the sudden, Peter flew behind a rock next to me. Peter is sixteen and he has charcoal black hair and brown eyes. He didn't see me, so I took advantage of that.

"Boo!" I jumped out by him. He flew up and started screaming. Ella came over to see her embarrassed younger brother and me laughing so hard I was crying.

"Did you scare him?" Ella started laughing with me.

"Yes!" My sides hurt. Everyone else came out from their hiding spots to see what happened to us. Poor Peter, I am sure he didn't expect me of all people to scare him. Oh well... "Sorry, Peter." I was still laughing at his reaction. He started laughing, too. We all talked and joked on the way home,

"Zipporah, that was pretty great, scaring Peter. He scares us all the time." Matthias stated.

"Why, thank you, it was quite funny..." I was starting to really like Matthias' company, a lot. We got back to the Taylor's house and my family had gone home because Leigh wasn't feeling well.

"If you want to stay for a little bit you can, your parents said that it was okay as long as you were back by dark. No later! " Tucker Taylor added with a not-so-friendly tone of voice.

"Okay, thank you, Mr. Taylor." I replied.

Ella and I went to her and her sister's room and played games and talked for a while.

"Can you believe that today was Paul and Mel's wedding? It feels like it was forever ago. I know it will feel empty without her." I spilled my thoughts to my new best friend.

"I bet that can be hard, I haven't had to experience that before. I'm guessing it won't be long until Matthias has a wife…he is a really great brother." Ella and I sat on her bed.

"He sure seems like it. When is your birthday?" I quickly changed the subject. "May second, when's yours…" we were cut off by Esther,

"We need to go, Zip. It's getting dark."

"See you later!" I told Ella. Esther and I walked home with the last light of sun leading our way.

Chapter Seven

Three months later a knock came to the door, I opened it to Matthias. *Brrr, it's getting cold out…* I thought.

"Hello, is your Pa home?" Matthias rubbed his hands together.

"Yes, he is in the barn." I answered.

"Okay, thanks." He turned and walked towards the barn. *Okay then…* I wondered what he wanted. *I guess it is none of my business.*

"Who was at the door?" Ma asked.

"Matthias Taylor." I answered and went to the kitchen. I swept the floor and hummed to myself. Another knock came to the door. I opened it to see Mel!

"Mel! Come in! I have hardly seen you since the wedding! I can't believe it has been three months..." I squeezed her tightly.

"Zipporah, I have to tell you something." Mel was extremely serious,

"Okay, what?" My mood quickly changed.

"I'm having a baby." she broke out in a smile.

"Mel!!! That's so exciting!" The door opened for a third time as we were hugging.

"What is so exciting?" Matthias asked. I looked at Mel, she looked at me.

"Nothing, did you find my Pa?" I asked him.

"You wanna go on a stroll with me?" I was definitely taken by surprise,

"Um—yes."

"I'll wait outside for you." Matthias walked out the door.

"Is there something I don't know about?" Mel turned to me.

"Not that I know of… yet." I put on my shawl and warm mittens and I walked out the door.

"Did I do something?" I asked Matthias.

"No." He started walking towards Liam and Emily's house, they live about a mile from our house so it took us a while. We went around their house. Not a word was said.

Lord, I don't know what is happening. I'm kind of afraid! We made it to a snow covered part of a hill. We were surrounded with pine trees, layered with a fresh blanket of snow. Matthias stopped and turned to me, he looked deep into my eyes.

"I have loved you ever since I drenched you with that water. I can't imagine my life without you." He got down on one knee, "Zipporah Ann, will you marry me?" He held out a beautiful ring, it had a gold band with a small heart on it. *Thank you, Lord.*

"Yes!" Tears filled my eyes.

"I'm glad you said yes!" Matthias joyfully said. "Do you know how much I have wanted this?" He smiled at me, took my hand, slipped my glove off and put on my ring.

"It's beautiful…" We walked back, my hand tightly in his.

"So this is why you went and talked with my Pa?" My curiosity got the best of me.

"Yes. Should we stop at Liam and Emily's house and tell them first?" My fiancé asked.

"Sure." We knocked on their door, Emily opened it.

"Oh!" She saw us holding hands. "Come in! Liam! Your sister is here! When did this happen?"

"About five minutes ago!" I joyfully said.

"I knew it! I told you Emily!" Liam walked into the room.

"How did you know?" Matthias asked.

"It was so clear, how could you not notice it?" He chuckled. "The giggles and the looks you two have exchanged over the past few months."

"When is the wedding?" Emily asked.

"We have not talked about that yet. I mean, it's December fourth, so maybe sometime January."

"How about December thirty-first?" Matthias threw out the idea.

"I would be okay with that. We will have to see if that works." I looked at my soon-to-be husband.

"We would love to stay and chat but we have to go tell the family... Oh! When do you want me to come and stay?" I asked Emily.

"Tomorrow?"

"Okay, see you then!" We left their house chatting all the way home. "What color should our wedding be?" I talked in excitement.

"Well, your favorite color is sapphire blue..."

"How did you know that?" I was shocked he knew little details about me.

"My sister is your best friend. I know your favorite color, your favorite bible verse, and you love little kids." He smirked.

"I don't know your answer to those questions." I confessed.

"Red, first Corinthians thirteen, and I do love kids. Now you know." He said with a smile.

"Ah, now I know. Thank you, Matthias." We exchanged smiles and continued on home.

Telling my family was great, even Mel was there to hear the news. *Twenty-seven days...* I thought. Matthias went home and agreed to come to supper tomorrow night at Liam and Emily's house.

"I am leaving tomorrow, all right?" I told my mother, who walked into the girls' room.

"Okay, hopefully she will have their baby soon!" Ma helped me pack a couple dresses in my bag to take.

"So, what do you think about this engagement?" Ma asked me.

"I'm really happy, why?"

"I thought you didn't like Matthias, after you met him."

"I didn't, but I guess God softened my heart. Matthias is a really great guy, I'm glad he proposed." I sat down next to Ma.

"He sure is, your Pa and I really like him too." She kissed my forehead and walked out of the room.

~~~

"Supper was amazing, thanks, Ladies." Liam said as he kissed his very pregnant wife on the head.

"I'll help with the dishes." Emily stood up.

"I don't think so, I will do them." I stood up and brought an armload of dishes to the sink.

"We can help her." Matthias jumped up and grabbed Liam.

"Oh… fine." Liam shook his head and let out a chuckle. "So, where are you planning on living?"

"My house." Matthias answered.

"You have a house?" I turned to him in confusion.

"Yes, I do. I built it in the summer and am finishing up the inside now." He smiled.

"Huh— where is it?" I asked him.

"It is not far from here. We walked past it on our walk." Matthias chuckled.

"That house was beautiful!" I was shocked! We quickly finished the dishes and Matthias had to go home. Three days passed. December seventh came. Emily had her babies. Twin girls, Amber and Adriel. We were all shocked it was twins. They both have dark hair and Amber has brown eyes and Adriel has blue eyes. My family and the Westly's (since Emily was their daughter) came over to see the twins. It was my turn to go home and Esther would stay with Emily.

Chapter Eight

"The wedding is five days away, we have pretty much everything ready, my dress, your suit, the bridesmaids' dresses, the men's suits, the church, the decorations, and the house. Are we forgetting anything?" I asked Matthias.

"Sounds like we have everything ready. Just think, in five days you will be Mrs. Zipporah Ann Taylor…" His voice trailed off.

"Okay, so, Liam, Paul, Thomas, and Noah are the groomsmen and Mel, Ella, Emily, and Lynn are the bridesmaids… So we need to have them ready in the morning because the wedding is at eleven o'clock." I mumbled under my voice.

"Don't worry, Zipporah. Everything will fall into place." Matthias relieved my stress. "Esther and Lynn are taking care of everything, right?" He looked at my two sisters sitting on the other side of the table.

"Yes, we have everything under control, Mel is coming over today to help finalize plans." Lynn reassured me.

"Good!" I smiled.

Later that day, Matthias, Eliza and I went on a walk. I asked him many questions about his past and he asked about mine, we talked about our dreams and decided that we will have as many kids as God wants us to have. Eliza followed a ways behind us, giving us privacy but also being a good chaperone and watching.

Four days until the wedding... I set out my clothes to pack and bring them over to our house.

"It's going to be so empty without you here." Lynn stated. Lynn and I have grown closer in the past few months, so it feels harder to leave. I know what she feels like, having a sister get married and leave.

"I know. I'll come over to visit and see you every Sunday at church." I hugged Lynn.

"You want to help me bring this over to Matthias' house?" I asked her.

"You mean your house?" She joked.

"Come on, silly." We got to my new house and started putting things in my new closet.

"I can't believe you get your own closet!" Lynn goofed around.

"I guess you have to get married first." I smirked and stuck my tongue out at her playfully. I heard Matthias come in with someone else.

"Pa! You can't have your way, I love Zipporah and you can't change me. I know this isn't what you want, but it is what I want. Be mad at me all you want, just don't you take this out on

Zipporah." Matthias was angry, I had never seen him so mad.

"Don't waste your time on some little town nobody. I will end up telling you, 'I told you so!' You could be in a big city, with a big job, and a beautiful, mature wife," Mr. Taylor snapped back at his son. My heart sank to my feet and I felt like crying, Lynn and I just sat there. We didn't say anything, how could we. I heard the door slam and I went out to the kitchen to look out the window. They were already gone, what was I supposed to do?

"Zipporah?" I turned to Matthias' voice. "Did you hear all that?"

"Yeah, and so did Lynn. What was that all about?" I was so confused and scared.

"My father and I just don't agree on anything, I promise, this changes nothing. I still love you, you mean everything to me, don't forget that." He pulled me close into his arms. "I love you, Zipporah." He whispered in my ear.

I thought a lot about what was said. I tried not to let it bother me and busied myself with the wedding.

Two days passed and tomorrow is the wedding. I hurried around and got the last minute things in place. *It's almost here…*

Lord, thank you for Matthias and for his love for me. I love him and I thank you for that, In Jesus name, Amen...

I finished praying and tidied up my things so I could get into bed. "Is anyone awake?" I whispered in my sister's room.

"We all are, we have been waiting for you." Esther sat up in her and Lynn's bed.

"You didn't have to wait for me." I got into bed.

"It's your last night as a Foxton lady, so we wanted to make sure you have a good last night." Eliza laughed. *My sweet, sweet sisters...* For quite a while we talked, laughed, and even cried a little. We all fell asleep and morning came quickly.

This is it! I jumped out of bed full of energy and jumped on my sister's beds like a child on Christmas morning.

"Today is the day! Who's excited?" I flew out of our room and ran down the stairs. Liam, Emily, Adriel, and Amber were already here.

"Someone is excited!" Emily laughed at me. I stopped in my tracks. I was still in my nightgown. *Oops.* I thought and ran back up the stairs.

Esther fixed my hair as the bridesmaids put on their sapphire blue dresses that my Mother, Lynn, and Eliza made. My hair was put up into a bun with a little braid and blue ribbon in it. I slipped my silk wedding dress on and had Mel tie it up.

"You are a beautiful bride." Emily told me.

The time had come. I stood with my arm on Pa's as the doors opened. I saw Matthias, our eyes locked; I couldn't help but smile. My sisters and best friend looked beautiful, and the men looked handsome, I could not believe my eyes when I saw Thomas; he looked like a man. My hands slipped into Matthias' hands, a tear slipped down my face; A happy tear. Pastor Cecil started with,

"Welcome to the wedding ceremony of Matthias Taylor and Zipporah Foxton. We gather here today to honor God." We had asked Pastor Cecil to do our wedding just like Paul and Mel's ceremony, but we wanted to write our own vows. Matthias' vow was:

Zipporah Ann, you are the love of my life, my best friend, and now you will be my wonderful wife. I am so beyond blessed that God made you to be my wife. I promise to love and encourage you, to lead you to God, and to be there for you always. You make me want to be a better man and to grow closer to God and further my relationship with our Father. I promise to raise our children in the Word of God and show them His ways. I promise to love you unconditionally. I Love you, Zipporah.

And this was mine:

Matthias Samuel, you are an answer to my parents, siblings, and my prayers. You are the man of God I know you are and you have taught me to love God even more. I promise to follow your instruction and be your wife until death do us part. Lord willing I will bear us children and we can raise them to know Jesus as their Savior. I love you so very much.

By the time we finished our vows we were both crying. We exchanged our rings and Pastor Cecil finished with,

"I now pronounce you Mr. and Mrs. Matthias Samuel Taylor." and before I knew it, he told Matthias he could kiss his bride, his cold hands touched my face and he pulled me in for our first kiss. We ran down the aisle, said our goodbyes and went to our new home.

"I love you, my wife." my husband said.

"And I love you, forever and always."

Chapter Nine

We pulled up to our new house, and I opened the door, before I knew what was happening Matthias picked me up and carried me over the threshold! I joyfully laughed as he set me down. We changed and got settled into our new cozy home.

"What do you want for supper?" I asked my husband.

"I don't care, something simple?"

"Eggs and toast it is!" I laughed.

"Isn't that breakfast?" He asked.

"Not anymore!" We finished supper and decided to go to bed.

"I stoked the fire, that should keep us warm tonight." He helped me make the bed.

"Good! As soon as you proposed I finished these quilts I'd been slowly working on for our bed."

"They look really wonderful. Good job, Love." He kissed my forehead and we climbed in bed. I woke up in the middle of the night to get some water. I walked out to the kitchen and there stood a giant silhouette of a man. I screamed. The man yelled and he quickly lit a candle. I broke out laughing to see Matthias standing there laughing also.

"What are you doing up?" He asked me.

"I was coming to get a drink, what are you doing up?" I sat at our kitchen table.

"I couldn't sleep so I was putting more wood on the fire…" His voice trailed off.

"I'm sorry, is there something I can do?" I grabbed his hand and looked into his eyes.

"You really wanna know what is bothering me?"

"Yes, I'm your wife, you can tell me anything."

"Sometimes when I get really excited, I don't sleep. I know, I know. It's silly." He blinked his heavy eyes.

"If it is important to you, it's important to me. And I understand, I still feel excited."

"Let's go back to bed, Love." He wrapped his arm around my shoulders and I wrapped mine around his waist.

A week later we went to church, of course my family and Matthias' family were there so that was great fun to see them again after the wedding. Liam and Emily invited us over for dinner, so after church we went to their house. Liam held Adriel and Matthias held Amber while Emily and I finished the dishes.

"Dinner was great. Thank you!" I told my sister-in-law.

"I'm glad you liked it!" We walked over and sat in the living room with the men. Matthias was making funny faces at Amber and she intently watched her new uncle.

"So, how is married life?" Liam asked.

"Great, everything I ever imagined, but more." I took Amber from Matthias and tried to help her not to cry.

"She is probably hungry." I handed Amber to her momma.

"It is definitely different than living with a family, it's just us two to worry about, for now." I smiled as Matthias wrapped his arm around me.

"Married life is such an amazing thing." Liam rocked his daughter.

"It sure is…" I leaned my head on my husband's shoulder. *How weird it is to be married now and be with Liam and Emily and their two daughters. Time sure has passed quickly…*

Our voices quietly continued on for a while until it was getting late.

"We better go, it is getting pretty dark." Matthias stood up from the couch we were sitting on. We stepped out into the cold. I shivered as we got into our carriage, Matthias took his blanket and put it over mine to keep me warm.

"You, Matthias Samuel, are a good husband."

"Well, I try my hardest. You do a pretty good job being a wife."

I giggled and blushed like a little girl from what Matthias said.

~~~

Four months had passed, married life was going pretty good, we had some hard bumps along the road, nothing too bad.

"Matthias, I can't make you supper, I feel terribly sick." I pitifully told him. He sat down next to me on the bed,

"Do you have a fever?" He touched my head. "You don't feel warm. Don't worry, I'll make something for us." He walked out of the room.

How do I tell him I'm pregnant? Should I just say, 'I'm pregnant!' No, I have to come up with something better... All of the sudden, I heard glass break. I jumped out of bed and flew to the kitchen to see Matthias picking up a broken plate.

"I accidently dropped this."

I just started to cry and I couldn't stop.

"It's just a broken plate, we can get another." Matthias was very confused.

"That was Grandfather Melford's favorite plate. I have not seen him in years, I wish he would come visit…" I sniffled.

"I'm sorry? Sweetheart." Confused, Matthias got up and hugged me. I continued to cry. I don't think Matthias was very used to having to be sympathetic to me.

That night we sat together in front of the fireplace. We didn't say much.

"Matthias, I have to tell you something…" He looked at me, "You're going to be more than my husband." He looked confused.

"What?"

"You are going to be a Father." He jumped out of his seat and picked me up and gave out a shout of joy!

"So that's why you were crying?" He asked after we settled down.

"I guess so." I joyfully laughed. The mood was completely changed from earlier. It's hard to believe I am growing a little gift from God in me. I've always prayed for children, and so had

Matthias. God had answered our prayers in many ways.

"Are you at all nervous, you know, about becoming a parent?" I asked Matthias a few nights later.

"Well, of course. But I know God has a plan for our little baby and He will show us what to do when the time comes for baby to enter the world. The bible says not to worry about tomorrow, let it worry about itself." He kissed my forehead and we went off to bed.

A couple weeks later, I was making supper and a knock came to the door. I opened it and leaped into the guest's arms. Grandfather Melford.

"Now look at you! As beautiful as ever."

"Awe! Papa Melford, I can't believe you are here!" I welcomed him into the house.

"Your husband sent me a telegram saying you missed me."

Matthias... I smiled at the thought of my husband.

"So you just came at the drop of a hat?" I asked papa Melford.

"He also said I could stay with you, aaand that your meals are pretty amazing, aaand it's almost your twenty first birthday...." He gave some pretty good reasons. I brought him to the guest room and went to finish supper before Matthias came home from work. He walked in to see me waiting right at the door.

"I can't believe you did this for me!" I jumped into his arms.

"Your grandfather came?" He smirked. "Your Pa and Ma are coming over for dessert later. I didn't tell them about Melford being here." He took off his coat and went to meet Papa Melford.

"Good to finally to meet you, Matthias."

"You too, Mr. Foxton." They shook hands.

"You call me Papa Melford, you're family now!" Papa laughed.

Later that night when my parents were coming over, Matthias pulled me aside,

"We should tell them tonight!" He could no longer hold it in. It was all he talked about since I told him!

"Okay, that's fine!" I gave him a quick kiss and went to watch my folk's expression of having Papa open the door.

"Come in!" Papa Melford said.

"Pa?" My father walked in and tightly hugged his Pa, he was overjoyed.

We sat and laughed and laughed around the dining room table.

"I can't wait to meet my great grandchildren..." Papa Melford leaned back in his chair. "I heard there are many now!"

"You sort of already have." Matthias looked at me.

"No way, you're not messing with us, are you?" Pa asked.

"In no way am I kidding."

Pa, Ma, and Papa Melford were shocked.

Later that night, Papa Melford stood in the kitchen with me as I did the dishes. He always had his two fingers tucked away in his pocket. Melford stood tall and slim. He is in his eighties and is mostly bald. I have very fond memories of him from when I was little and when I would go to his house and he would give us each little cookies.

"Papa, can I ask you something?" I looked at him.

"Sure, Hun, what is it?" Papa Melford asked.

"I-um-what do you think of Matthias?" I blurted out my question. I respected what my Papa was about to say.

"Well, I just met him. He seems like a good guy. I think we will get along swell."

"Thanks Papa." I gave him a squeeze and went off to bed.

"Night, Zipporah." Papa said as I turned the corner to go into my room.

Chapter Ten

Spring was in the air and I went out on a walk with Papa Melford after Matthias and I finished our devotions.

"Zipporah, I think I need to go back home." Papa Melford stated.

"I don't want you to go." I stopped and looked at him.

"I have decided to move back here. I'm going back for a couple weeks to sell what I have and come build a small house here." Papa chuckled.

"I'm so glad you are staying!" I wrapped my arms around him. In the distance, I could see Mel and Paul walking our way.

"Hello! Out on a stroll?" I kept walking towards them. Apparently, word had not yet reached Paul and Mel that Papa was here visiting, they had not been to church in the past month because she was feeling ill. Mel squinted her eyes at us walking together.

"Papa Melford?" She stood still.

"Amelia." He tipped his hat and went and hugged his granddaughter.

"What are you doing here?" Mel didn't know what to say.

"I've been here for the last few days, staying with your sister. I heard you were sick and didn't want to give you company unexpectedly."

"You are welcome at my house anytime." She hugged Papa again. "Oh! This is my husband, Paul Westly. Paul, this is Papa Melford."

"Nice to meet you, Papa Melford." Paul stood about as tall as Papa, he has a slim build and has a dark beard now. The four of us kept on walking.

"Paul," I turned to my brother-in-law. "Is Matthias helping you tomorrow with plowing your field after doing ours?" I asked.

"Yeah, I'm heading over to your field after this."

Late that night, Matthias walked in. I was sitting, waiting for him to come in.

"You're still up? You should be asleep!" His voice arose.

"I just wanted to make sure you came in. Don't be angry!" I stood up to him.

"I'm not!" He yelled. I got quiet, I knew something happened and he was not telling me. I watched him walk over to the kitchen, he was limping.

"What happened?" My eyes filled with tears.

"Paul was running the plow and I was walking next to it, a piece of wood flew off and cut my leg. I'm fine." He swallowed hard.

"What's really going on?" All of the sudden, someone was rapidly knocking on the door. Matthias opened it to his sister, Ella, she flew into his arms.

"What's wrong?" He held his younger sister close.

"They...are...leaving...!" She managed to get out the words between sobs.

"Who is leaving?" He asked.

"P-p-p-pa and m-m-ma and the kids." She was not crying as hard as before. Another knock came to the door.

"Ella! Are you in there?" Tucker Taylor yelled.

"Please! don't make me leave you!" She begged her older brother. Matthias turned to me,

"You and Ella go into our room, I'll handle Pa."

We quickly ran off into our room. We could hear Matthias and his Pa angrily talking.

"Matthias has always been there for me when Pa was not, I don't want to leave him." Ella said.

"So what's the problem between Matthias and his Pa?" I curiously asked.

"When we lived in South Dakota, Pa really pushed marriage on Matthias, he tried to get him to marry this one girl, Viola, and Matthias said that he wants God to choose his wife. They have never really got along since, they just kind of pretend to be okay. There is much more to the story, but it would take me all day. Pa has had somewhat of a drinking problem." She blurted out.

"Oh my..." was all I could say.

We finally crawled into bed, it was late and I just wanted to sleep. I didn't want to talk to Matthias, not after what happened tonight.

"You awake, Zip?" Matthias turned over to see me.

"Sort of, why?" I tried to fight off the sleep that was calling.

"Thank you." Matthias blurted out.

"For what?"

"Just letting Ella stay and I feel bad for burdening you with this problem between my Pa and I." Matthias sadly said.

"The day I said 'I do' made me part of you. I don't want you to feel bad for this, and Ella made a really hard decision. Ella also told me what happened between you two." I looked at Matthias.

"I'm sorry for not telling you, you should have known. I should have just told you before we were married." He hugged me.

"The past is the past, you or I can't change it. I am not upset, it's just that I thought your Pa was different. I guess I was wrong."

"I know... we better get some sleep." Matthias kissed me and turned over.

"Wait, Matthias, what were you angry about before Ella came to the door?" I asked.

"I was having a hard time with Pa, I tried talking with him, it was like talking to a brick wall. I shouldn't have taken it out on you, I'm sorry."

I started to pray out loud.

"Lord, Please help Matthias and Ella, they are in pain from what their father did, and I thank you for Your help already. And help Tucker Taylor..."

~~~

Morning came and Matthias went to his family's house to try and mend things before they left. Ella and Papa Melford came out from their rooms, Papa heard a little talking but didn't get up, he was confused why my husband's sister was here. I explained it to him while I made breakfast,

"And I missed all that?" Papa Melford asked.

"Yep, it was not pretty, poor Matthias and Ella. Matthias went to go talk with his Pa right now, hopefully that goes well." I whisked the eggs together as I waited for Matthias to return.

Shortly after breakfast was done, Matthias came in and walked straight to our room. I stood up from the table and went to find him. "How did it go?" I went and sat next to my husband.

"My Pa is an angry man, he is leaving…He was drunk last night when he came over." He buried his face with his hands and wept. I could not believe this was happening. Tucker was mean, and he was afraid to face his problems. He just runs from them, and the worst part is that his family has to run with him. I couldn't imagine if that was my father. I just sat with my arms around my husband. I didn't feel like I could say or do anything to help with this pain.

A while later, we went out and ate cold eggs.

"Ella," Matthias looked at his sister, "If you want, you can stay with us or leave with Pa."

"I already know what God wants me to do. He wants me to stay here, I don't want to leave my siblings, but I have to."

Chapter Eleven

Papa Melford decided that it was time to head back and sell his things.

"See you in a while, take care of that precious cargo." He hugged me. "And you, take care of them. She is pretty special." He shook Matthias' hand.

"Will do, safe travels." We watched Papa Melford ride off.

The sun set and we were out on a walk, just the two of us.

We stopped once the sun was gone. It was late May. We found a dry spot of grass and laid stargazing.

"I can't wait for our baby..." Matthias put his hand on my little baby bump.

"It is hard to wait, that is for sure. I think Mel is going to have her baby any day now."

"I just want him or her here fast. Are you going to help Mel?" He asked.

"I want baby here, too. I don't know...I might help her, if she wants."

The next morning, Paul came running in. "It's Mel, she is having the baby!" He said very out of breath.

"Okay, I'm coming!" Matthias was not awake yet so I ran into our room.

"Love," I whispered. "I have to go help with Mel's birth." I told him and left. I got to Mel's house, Esther was there too and her delivery went very smoothly. I carried out a little boy to his new Pa.

"You now have a son..." I set Paul's baby boy in his arms, tears of joy filled Paul's eyes.

"Can I see Mel?" He asked.

I nodded my head, "Yes, you can."

He walked into their room, they both laughed and even cried a little.

"We are naming him Abraham." Mel told us. Esther said I could leave because Ma was coming. Right before I went to go out the door Esther stopped me.

"I was wondering if I could help with your birth?" She asked.

Of course! That would be amazing!" I hugged my sister. We said our goodbyes and I went back home. I walked in to Ella and Matthias eating lunch,

"Oh! Thank you, Ella." I sat down as she put food on my plate.

"Did Mel have her baby?" Matthias asked. "Yes, she had a baby boy. They named him Abraham."

After lunch, I went to our room and laid down. *I'm so tired.* I thought.

"You sleeping?" Matthias whispered.

"No, just tired. What do you need?"

"I was thinking we could make a list of possible names for our baby." He requested.

"Okay, grab some paper and pencil and we will start it." I sat up on our bed.

"What do you think about Freda-Ford?" Matthias offered his thought.

"No way. That's one I will not name my child...How about you make a list and I make a list and after supper we will look at each other's." I mentioned the thought.

"If we pick names, we can always change it," my husband said.

"Oh, my! I just remembered that Eliza, Leigh, and Thomas are coming over for supper." I blurted out my forgotten thoughts.

"Ella and I will make steak and potatoes for supper. And for a special dessert, I made rhubarb and strawberry pie." I told Matthias as he brought my younger siblings in.

"Zippy!" Thomas ran up and hugged me.

"I missed you Tommy!" I told him. We sat down and prayed, then we ate. Eliza, Leigh, and Thomas told us all the happenings at Pa and Ma's house.

"And we are getting a dog!" Leigh added to our conversation.

"No, we are not getting a dog. He just wants a dog." Eliza stated. I didn't realize how much I had missed the youngest three. We finished supper and we went to bring the threesome home.

"How are you feeling?" My mother asked me.

"Tired, I've been so busy. And very soon I will have to plant a garden. I'm sure Ella will be a huge help, she always helps with anything…" Before my mother could say anything else, Matthias interrupted us,

"Love, we really should go, it's getting late." He wrapped his arm around my waist.

"Why don't you come over tomorrow?" I asked my mother.

"Okay, how about after lunch?"

"Perfect" I gave her a quick hug and went out the door.

"Have your list ready? I do." Matthias smirked.

"Of course I do, silly. Did you put them in order of how much you like the names?" I raised my eyebrows.

"Yes, I did."

"I'm very surprised…" We got home and sat by the fire.

"I think I'm going to go to bed, I'm exhausted," Ella said.

"Okay, goodnight." I told her.

"Ready?"

I knew Matthias was talking about the list. We both went and got ours.

"Here is mine." He gave me his list.

Matthias' list of names

Boy names:

Ralph

Daniel

Girl names:

Grace

Erica

Zipporah's list

Ralph   Opal

Jack   Randalynn

Melford   Elizabeth

"We both picked 'Ralph' for a boy name!" I laughed. "I don't really like some of those names all too much."

"What about Ralph Melford for the boy name?" Matthias suggested. I thought for a second.

"I like that, a lot." *Ralph Melford…*

"What about for the girl's name?" He asked. "I love the name Opal, I always have."

"We could do Grace Opal."

"Really? No, that is silly! It should be Opal Grace, that would flow off the tongue much smoother." I stated.

"I don't know about that…" Matthias ran his fingers through his dark brown hair.

"You think that is a bad name?" I asked.

"I didn't say bad, I just don't know," Matthias firmly said.

"Okay. I'll let it grow on you," I laughed.

Chapter Twelve

"Come in!" I opened the door for my mother. She came into the room with a plate of my favorite pie, apple.

"You brought pie!" I exclaimed.

"I have hardly got to see you lately, so I thought I would treat you." She sat the warm apple pie on the table.

"We can sit in the living room if you want." I mentioned to my mother.

"Okay. I have only been in your house a couple times, I forget how much I like it!" Ma looked around my living room.

"You know you're always welcome to stop in whenever, right? Pa can, too. And thank you, it's finally how I like it." I rocked in my rocking chair.

"So, Ella is living here?" Ma asked.

"Yes, for now she is. I'm guessing she will for a while…"

"What if she came and lived with us until after you have the baby?"

"I'd have to talk to Matthias and Ella. I'll tell you what we decide," I responded.

"For the sake of your marriage, you need some time alone. You have had Papa Melford, then Ella." My Mother was right.

"I know, but Ella had to make a really hard choice and she chose to stay with us. We can't just kick her out." I said.

"I know, it's a hard choice. Just think about it." We ate pie and then Ma had to go home and start supper. Around the dinner table, I thought I should ask Matthias and Ella what they thought of the idea.

"Well, what do you think, Ella?" Her brother asked.

"That would be nice to stay with them for a while, I miss having younger kids around. And as long as I can come back and visit." She smiled.

"I'll let my Ma know." I finished the food on my plate and brought the dishes to the sink.

It was now the middle of June and it was really hot outside. My baby bump was sticking out pretty far now, I am due around the beginning of September.

"I can wash the dishes tonight." Ella took the plate out of my hand.

"You don't have to..." I replied, but she did them anyways. A knock came to the door and Matthias opened it to Pa.

"Hello, did y'all finish supper?"

"Yep, we sure did… Come on in."
Matthias opened the door wider for Pa to come in.

"Is Zipporah here?" I got up from my chair and walked to the entry room,

"Yes, I am!"

"Your Ma wanted me to drop this off to you on my way by." He handed me a letter.

"Thanks Pa. I made some cookies if you would like to join us for dessert." I asked.

"Don't mind if I do!" We walked over to the table and I grabbed the cookies.

"Mm— tastes delicious, Zip." Pa helped himself to another cookie.

"Thanks, it's Ma's recipe. I think hers are better…"

"I have had your Ma's cookies, it's a close tie." Matthias joined the conversation.

"I gotta run, I have a couple things to do before it gets dark. Thanks again for the cookies, Zip." Pa walked toward the door.

"Anytime! And tell Ma that we will have Ella stay with you guys for a while." I hugged my Pa and he left. *I wonder what the letters about…* I opened it to a small card:

Dear Zipporah,

Thank you so much for making time for me. I really enjoyed it! I just wanted to send you some encouragement as you are getting ready for your first baby. Get <u>lots</u> of sleep now, be open to help, and pray for your little baby!

Love,

Ma

"What are you doing tomorrow?" Matthias asked as I set the letter down.

"Make meals, clean, maybe work on the baby quilt... Why?" I curiously asked.

"It is your twenty-first birthday." Matthias stated.

"Oh my! I almost forgot! June seventeenth is my birthday... how did I not remember!" I rubbed my head. "Don't worry about it, Zipporah. I have the whole day planned out." Matthias wrapped his arms around me.

"Really? That's so sweet!"

~~~

"Wake up, Love." Matthias kissed my sleeping head.

"Why?" I hardly opened my eyes.

96

"Because it is your birthday, and breakfast is ready." My eyes opened further,

"Seriously?"

He nodded his head 'yes.'

"Okay, I'll be down in a second. Did Ella help you?" I asked.

"She went to your parents this morning, so it could just be us today."

"Really? Aww..." We walked into the kitchen and I could smell cinnamon rolls, one of my favorite breakfasts.

"Aww, this is so sweet." I sat at the table. It had a pretty green table cloth with little purple flowers and he had daisies in a vase. I enjoyed my breakfast and went to get dressed after Matthias insisted on doing the dishes. I slipped a purple dress on and went back out to the kitchen.

"I'm almost done!" Matthias huffed. "I don't know how you keep up with all these dishes, three times a day!"

"Just washing two or three people's dishes is nothing, think about having six, seven, or eight family members to wash dishes for..." I raised my eyebrows at him.

"Ah, that would be a lot of work. So after this, we will go on a walk and then Paul and Mel invited us over for cake, she said that some of your family will be there too." Matthias dried his hands.

"Okay." *How did I get to be so blessed with Matthias as a husband...* I thought as we walked out the door. The walk was beautiful, I was extremely hot, especially carrying this extra weight around.

"Ready to head to Mel's?" Matthias could tell I was struggling.

"Yeah, I'm ready..." We walked to their house and my family was already there, with cake and gifts. "Aww! You shouldn't have!" I went around the room hugging each family member. I came to someone I didn't know. "I don't think we have met..." My voice trailed off as I stood face to face with a strange man.

"I'm John, Esther's friend."

"Oh, I have not heard anything about you. But it's nice to meet you!" I turned to Esther and gave her the 'sister' look saying 'why didn't you tell me?' and she just smiled back. We sat around the living room and Thomas brought me some gifts. I pulled the first gift open, it was beautiful pot holders handmade by my mother. I opened another gift, it was an amazing drawing of me and Matthias in a frame, "Who did this?" I looked around the room.

"Eliza did it." Leigh spoke up.

"Eliza, this is so beautiful! You did an amazing job!"

"Thanks." She blushed a little. Next I opened up a book, it was a journal. It had a beautiful leather binding and a pretty cover. I finished opening my gifts and we had chocolate cake.

We went late into the night talking, we finally went home. I slipped into my nightgown and sat on the porch. Matthias grabbed me a blanket and came and sat with me. I pulled out my journal and wrote my first entry.

June 17th

Today was my birthday and I was so surprised by everything Matthias did for me. I look back on the past year and how much my life has changed, a husband, and now and little baby on the way. I really love it all. I can't wait to see what the next year holds for us three.

Write more soon!

I set down my book and pencil and watched Matthias as he said,

"I have something for you." He handed me a small box. "Open it." I opened the box to a beautiful necklace with one pearl on it.

"Every time you are going to have a baby, I'll add a pearl." He said.

"That's so beautiful!" My heart melted.

"I love you, Zipporah Ann Taylor."

Chapter Thirteen

Over a month had passed since my birthday and it was August twenty-fifth. I stood in the kitchen making breakfast and felt like baby Taylor was on the way.

"Matthias!" I shouted in pain, he came running to my side.

"What's wrong?" He asked.

"I think it's the baby, it hurts so bad!" I screamed.

"What do you want me to do?" He started to panic.

"Get... Esther..." He helped me to our room and left. *The pain! It hurts so bad, I can hardly stay still.* My hands were shaking and I started to cry out to God to help me. *Lord! I'm in pain! Please protect the baby... and me!*

Esther and Matthias burst through the door and Esther came into our room. She felt my stomach, "You will have this baby soon, I promise." She hurried around to get things ready for the baby. Time passed, a minute felt like an hour. "You are almost there!" Esther encouraged me,

"Is she okay?" My helpless husband stood outside the door.

"Here baby comes!" Esther yelled over my shouts of pain. Waaaa! The baby is here, a sigh of relief came out of my mouth.

"Don't tell me the gender, I want to wait for Matthias." I said.

"Okay, let me clean your baby up and then I'll let him in." Esther worked quickly and let Matthias in, he came and sat on the bed next to me.

"You have a daughter!" She handed our precious daughter to me.

"Opal Grace…" Matthias touched Opal's tiny pink face.

"I can't believe she is here, praise God." I held my daughter.

"I'll be back in a little bit, I think Ella is coming over to help." Esther cleaned up and left.

A while later, Ella came over.

"Esther wouldn't tell us what you had. She said you probably wanted to tell me…" She told Matthias,

"We had a girl, Opal Grace…"

"Aww!" I passed Opal to her. "She is so beautiful!"

"Thank you, she gets her good looks from me." Matthias jokingly pumped his chest out.

"I'll start on supper." Ella went out of our room. "You did a great job, Zip. I'm so proud of you!" Matthias kissed my forehead.

"With God all things are possible, right?" I smiled at my husband.

"'May there be pain in the night, but joy comes in the morning,'" Matthias recited.

"Psalms thirty: five," I replied. Later that night Pa, Ma, Esther, Eliza, Thomas, and Leigh came over. The first thing that was said was by Leigh,

"That baby looks like a potato..."

Everyone just busted out laughing.

"Well, it is a girl potato," I joked.

"What did you name her?" Ma asked.

"Opal Grace," Matthias answered.

"She is so adorable!" They stayed for a while, taking turns holding the new grandbaby and then they left.

"Would you stop at Mel's and tell her I had the baby and that she can come visit?" I asked.

"Sure." I sat in bed that evening, I just held Opal as she slept. Matthias stayed close by, just watching and talking with me.

"You want to hold her?" I asked.

"Does a new father want to hold his daughter?" He rolled his eyes at me.

"Here." I laughed!

"She is so precious…" He put his finger in her little hand.

"I know, it feels like she is not ours, like she is one of my siblings," I stated.

"We have started our own little family now." He started laughing.

"What?" I asked.

"I was just thinking about when we first met…"

"I never wanted to see your face again, now all I want is to see you…"

"I felt so bad about soaking you." He laughed again.

"Then I married you!" I grabbed my Journal and opened it to a surprise,

Aug. 25th

Hi there, Matthias here.

You had our baby this morning! You did such a great job. I know you will make a great mother for our little baby girl. I hope she grows up to be just like you and look the same too. I praise God each day for you, I love you.

-Matthias

What a sweetheart... I thought.

~~~

"I'm back!" Papa Melford walked in the door.

"Papa!" I hugged him,

"How did moving go?" I asked.

"Great, this time I will stay with your sister, Amelia, or as y'all call her Mel. Then when I get my house built, I'll move in there." He chuckled. Opal started to cry so I went to go get her.

"You're not pregnant anymore, are you?" Papa Melford said.

"Nope, I'll go get your great granddaughter!" I joyfully laughed.

"Grand-daughter, huh." I heard Papa Melford say.

106

"Meet Opal Grace." I laid Opal in his arms.

"Opal Grace, what a sweet name…" He rocked her back and forth.

"Is Ella still staying with y'all?" Papa Melford asked.

"She is now. She was staying with Ma and Pa," I replied.

"Huh—did Matthias' Pa leave?" He asked.

"Yes, he did. I think it still bothers Matthias…" My voice trailed off.

"I'm still praying about that. God will fix things."

"I hope so, Matthias has never gotten along with his Pa anyways."

Opal started to cry again.

"She needs to eat…" I took her from Papa.

"How long ago did you have her?"

"She was born last month."

"Aww, she is just brand new!" Papa Melford chuckled.

Chapter Fourteen

Months passed by with having little Opal, nothing exciting really happened until today.

"Storm's coming…" Matthias walked into the door.

"Rain?" I asked.

"Yeah, it's getting real dark out there." He looked very serious.

"Okay." I went about washing the floor.

"I saw Ella today, she was out on a walk so I talked to her for a bit," Matthias said.

"That's nice, what's she up to?" I asked.

"She has been getting letters from Peter." He looked at me.

"Really?"

"Peter said Pa is trying to send a husband to Ella. He makes me so upset…" Matthias rubbed his frustrated hand through his dark brown hair.

"Boy oh boy. What are you going to do?" I asked.

"I don't know what I can do…" He shook his head.

"Pray about it," I said.

"I know, it's so hard to pray without ceasing. I'm trying…"

This has to be so hard for Matthias, I know it is. It is even hard on me. I thought. "I have to watch out for any 'newcomers' in town, I guess." Matthias went back to the door.

"I'll be back in time for supper, I am just going to tell your Pa what's going on." He left and I turned to Opal,

"Poor Daddy..." Opal started to cry as if she knew what was going on. "I know, I know. Don't cry." I told her with sympathy.

It was soon getting dark and it started to rain. *I hope Matthias comes back soon...* I started to get worried. Time went by, still so sign of my husband. *Lord, protect Matthias, please!* I cried.

It was pitch black out and pouring rain; the rain started to lighten up and I sat up with sleeping Opal in my arms. *Where is he?* I thought. Suddenly I saw a candle light coming toward the house. I laid Opal down in her crib and ran to the door. I opened it to Liam.

"What are you doing here?" I asked.

"Good to see you to, Sis."

"Sorry, I just have been waiting for Matthias to get home. I'm really worried about him!" I cried.

"He is at my house, he slipped in the field and twisted his ankle. He is okay, I just needed to tell you."

"Oh, no! Poor Matthias... Can I come with you back to your house?"

"You can't bring Opal into the rain. The rain is going to start again soon."

"So I have to stay here all alone?"

"Yeah, just for tonight." Liam said.

"And you are leaving?"

"Yeah… I'll be back in the morning." He walked out of the house. *Lord, please protect us. I'm so scared and I don't even like the rain!* I silently prayed.

~~~

Morning came and we were still sleeping. I felt someone touch my shoulder and I jumped awake. Matthias was home, what a relief.

"Are you okay?" I rubbed my eyes.

"Yeah, it's just a small twist. I'm fine." He crawled into bed next to me and Opal.

"I'm so glad you're home. I was so scared."

"I know, Liam told me you didn't want to stay alone."

"I didn't want to. That was the first time I have ever stayed alone. I had Opal with me but she's a baby, so…"

"I'm here now, and my ankle is just fine."

I got out of bed and fed Opal, she was now nine months old. After I finished, I started making breakfast. Matthias came and took Opal from my arms and went to play with her. I could hear joyous laughing coming from both of them as they stuck their tongues out at each other. Then they slowly stopped making noise.

I finished breakfast and went to get them but they both were sleeping on the floor. Opal laid on Matthias' chest and Matthias laid on the floor. *I can't leave these two together for too long!* I laughed to myself. Matthias finally woke up and came for breakfast.

"I got busy..." He smiled as he sat at the table.

"It's okay!" We prayed and ate. While I was doing the dishes, Opal sat on the floor with Matthias next to me.

"Who is that?" Matthias asked Opal. "Who is it?" He asked again.

"Mama," Opal said as she clapped her hands together. I turned my head in shock.

"Her first word!" We happily exclaimed.

"Mama," Opal said it again.

"What? My little girl!" I laughed.

Chapter Fifteen

"Happy birthday to you!" Matthias and I sang to little Opal.

"I cannot believe she's one!" I stated.

"I can't either…"

"Pa-pa," Opal said.

"What?" He smiled.

"Ma-ma."

"What, sweetheart?"

"Pa-pa, Ma-ma." Opal giggled.

"What a sweet little girl!" Matthias chuckled at our daughter.

"Your Uncle Liam, Aunt Emily, Adriel, Amber, Uncle Paul, Aunt Mel, Abraham, Papa Melford, and Aunt Ella are coming over tonight!" I told Opal, she started clapping her hands.

"Your family isn't coming?" Matthias asked.

"No, they went on a little trip together. They are probably coming over tomorrow or something."

"Okay."

Right before everyone came, I pulled Matthias aside.

"I'm pregnant." I said.

"What? Seriously?!"

"Yes!" He picked me off my feet and swung me around.

"Now, we won't tell anyone today, I want to wait for my family to come."

"It will be so hard to not say anything," Matthias said.

"I know, but we should not say anything." I shook my finger at him.

"Ah... fine." My husband laughed.

Family started to come and it was a fun time. Opal laughed at her silly family. Adriel and Amber were 'helping' her open her gifts, what can you expect from two-year-olds? Abraham sat quietly and watched them, he was the only boy cousin.

A knock came to the door and I went to get it.

"Pa! Ma!" I said as I hugged my Pa, "What are you doing here? I thought you were not getting home until tomorrow!"

"We ended up coming home early because we wanted to come to the party!" Ma smiled.

"I'm so glad you made it!" I welcomed them in. The room was filled with chatter and laughter.

"Opal!" Thomas laughed at his little niece stealing his cake. I went and took her from Thomas' lap and brought her over to Matthias.

"Now that your parents are here." He raised his eyebrows at me.

"Okay, let's have Opal tell them." I went to Opal's room and grabbed her baby doll.

"What is this?" I asked Opal in front of everyone. "Babeeeee" She giggled.

"And who am I?"

"Mama!"

"Mama, baby." I whispered to her.

"Mama, Babeeeee!" She kept laughing.

"What are you saying, Zipporah?" Eliza asked.

"You know what we are saying…" Everyone broke out in joyful shouts, *it is so fun telling people the news!* I thought.

Later that night, I laid in bed and waited for Matthias.

"What a fun night…" He crawled into bed.

"It was fun! I wish your parents were here to see Opal." I sighed.

"Me too, it's a bummer. I'm still having a hard time with that…"

"I'm sorry."

"I love you, Mrs. Taylor." He kissed me and I quickly fell asleep.

~~~

"Is anyone home?" A man's voice came from outside. I rushed to the door and I opened it.

"Tucker Taylor? What a surprise!" I nervously said.

"Zipporah, Is Matthias here?" He asked. Opal started to cry.

"Whose baby is that?"

"Matthias and I had Opal Grace one year ago, yesterday. And I am expecting again." I let him inside. I could tell something was the matter when he turned to me with heavy eyes. I felt really weird, why was he here? What did he want? What should I do?

"Zipporah, I owe you a huge apology, I understand if you can't forgive me for my wrong-doings and terrible words and behavior towards y'all." He swallowed hard.

"Of course, I can forgive you. You didn't hurt me as much as you hurt Matthias and Ella. They have really had a hard time since you left and they might have a hard time forgiving you," I boldly said.

"I understand..." He was cut off by Matthias coming in the back door.

"Pa?" Matthias looked at his father. "Why are you here?"

"Matthias, I'm so, so sorry. I did wrong. I asked God to forgive me, and now I'm asking you to forgive me," Tucker said with all his heart.

"Are you still upset that I married Zipporah?" Matthias asked.

"No, you were right to have God choose your wife, not me," Tucker said.

"Are you still upset with Ella?" Matthias wanted to make sure that he was fully changed.

"No, I was in the wrong."

Silence filled the room as Matthias thought of his answer.

"Yes, I forgive you. It will still take time to mend things, though." He hugged his Pa.

"You are a good son, Matthias. I wish I was like you."

"Do you want to meet your granddaughter?" Matthias quickly changed the conversation.

"Of course!" Mr. Taylor played with Opal for a while then said, "I need to go talk with your sister. I'll see you at church tomorrow." He stood up and walked out.

"God is so good..." I heard Matthias whisper.

"He sure is."

Chapter Sixteen

"Honey?" Matthias called from the living room.

"Yes, dear?"

"I am going to run into town, do you need anything?" Matthias came into the kitchen.

"No, I don't think so. Are you taking Opal with you?"

"Sure, I think she would like that!" Matthias scooped up our little daughter and off they went. I kept myself busy while my husband and daughter ran errands together. I finished my cleaning and grabbed my journal and sat down to write.

Today has been good, I've been keeping myself busy with cleaning and taking care of Opal. I have felt pretty well, not much for morning sickness, just starting to feel a little sleepy. Matthias has been a big help around here.

Nothing really has been going on lately, I think we might go over to Pa and Ma's house tonight for supper after Matthias and Opal come back.

I set down my pencil and book and walked to the bedroom, *maybe just a little nap…* I thought as crawled into the bed. The next thing I remembered was hearing a crash in the other room, I jumped out of bed and went flying to the kitchen. Matthias looked at me,

"Sorry, I just dropped a piece of wood for the stove. Did I wake you?"

"Yes, it's okay. Where is Opal?" I looked around the room to see it was baby-less.

"I dropped her off at your parent's house, I told them I would come and get you." Matthias threw the log into the stove.

"Okay, I'll fix my hair and then we can go." I turned to head for the bedroom but stopped to Matthias voice calling my name. "Yes?"

"I got a letter from my brother."

"Good, what did he say?" I asked.

"He said that there are some open jobs with the railroad up in Minnesota, He ended up not going with my Pa when he left here. I guess he ended up in Minnesota. He asked if I would be interested in coming and helping him for a couple months. You and Opal could stay here, or you could come with... I don't know, he said that there would be a lot of money in it and a lot to learn."

"Well... I think it would be a great job for you, with your work being slow right now, maybe we should. Baby won't be born until sometime in April."

"You are really okay with this? I am asking a lot here!" Matthias questioned my quick decision.

"Yes, if this is what needs to be done, then we will go to Minnesota. Of course I will miss my family and all our friends here. But, we will be back soon—it is only a couple months!"

I truly don't think it should be that big of a problem, I know Matthias just wants the best for us. I thought.

"Before we go any further into this conversation, I think we should stop and do what we should have done in the first place, pray about it. Let God decide, not us." We sat and prayed together and I left to fix my hair.

Pulling up to my parent's house brought back old memories as I watched Eliza, who is now very much grown up, and my daughter play. It reminded me of myself and Eliza when she was little. Life is different now, and I sure do like it.

Matthias and I decided to not say anything to my family that night—especially since we were not sure of what God's plan for us is yet.

Once we got home, I went and sat by Matthias on the bed. He had his Bible in his lap, I peered over his shoulder to see he had it open to Psalms one hundred and twenty-one, my favorite chapter.

"Have you thought any at all about Minnesota?" I asked.

"Yes, God has really given me peace about it. If you are ready, we will go."

I was nervous and excited all at one time, Matthias said that in the morning he would go into town and book the train ticket and send a letter to his brother. We would leave in one week.

One week can fly by, fast. With our trunks next to us, we said our 'goodbyes' to both of our families. I pulled out my journal and wrote once we got on the train,

Oct 9th

We just boarded the train. I thought it would be hard to say goodbye to my family but somehow it was not. I know that Minnesota will be different and maybe somewhat of a challenge, but I know God will help us through it, He always does, and I know He always will.

Opal Grace has been growing like a weed, she is such a small little bundle of joy. I don't know where I would be without her.

I will write more soon, once we get to Minnesota.

I set down my journal and quickly fell asleep as I watched Matthias and Opal play together.

"Sweetheart, we are getting close." Matthias patted my shoulder.

"Really?" I looked out the window to see a light snow covering the beautiful pine and spruce trees. *Wow… It is so wonderful!* I thought.

I grabbed Matthias' hand as we took our first steps in this new, undiscovered land that we could call our home for the next couple months.

Suddenly, I felt scared and worried. *Why did we decide to do this? It is so foolish, what were we thinking?*

"I am scared, Matthias." I whispered into my husband's ear.

"Me too, but I know God will take care of us in our adventure…"

Meet the Author!

Madisen M. Bourman is a Minnesota based Christian fiction author. Being home-educated, she learned to love writing short stories as a child. In Madisen's free time, she loves reading, traveling, baking, four-wheeling, music, sewing, playing with her two dogs, and hunting.

Find Madisen's blog at:
felicitousdayblog.blogspot.com

Letter from the author:

Hello reader!

Thank you so much for reading my first self-published book. It definitely took a lot of work to make it, but it was totally worth every minute of it. I didn't know much about self-publishing until I found Bethany Atazadah and Kristen Martin on Youtube. They have so many great tips and videos about self-publishing on their YouTube channels. If you are interested in self-publishing, I would say you should do it. It has really been so wonderful! I used KDP to design the cover and print my book.

Also, thank you to my friend, Amanda Grace Hage, for fully editing it. She has been such a great mentor to me, a new author. I absolutely love her books and they are such great stories.

Made in the USA
Middletown, DE
28 November 2018